Little Bad Riding Hood

Written by Julia Jarman

Illustrated by Jane Cope

Crabtree Publishing Company

www.crabtreebooks.com

Crabtree Publishing Company
www.crabtreebooks.com
1-800-387-7650

PMB 59051, 350 Fifth Ave.
59th Floor,
New York, NY 10118

616 Welland Ave.
St. Catharines, ON
L2M 5V6

Published by Crabtree Publishing in 2014

Series editor: Melanie Palmer
Editor: Crystal Sikkens
Notes to adults: Reagan Miller
Series advisor: Catherine Glavina
Series designer: Peter Scoulding
Production coordinator and
  Prepress technician: Margaret Amy Salter
Print coordinator: Margaret Amy Salter

Text © Julia Jarman 2010
Illustrations © Jane Cope 2010

First published in 2010
by Franklin Watts
(A division of Hachette
Children's Books)

Printed in
Canada/022014/MA20131220

Library and Archives Canada
Cataloguing in Publication

Jarman, Julia, author
        Little bad riding hood / written by Julia
Jarman ; illustrated by Jane Cope.

(Tadpoles: fairytale twists)
Issued in print and electronic formats.
ISBN 978-0-7787-0442-3 (bound).--ISBN 978-0-7787-
0450-8 (pbk.).--ISBN 978-1-4271-7562-5 (pdf).--ISBN
978-1-4271-7554-0 (html)

        I. Cope, Jane, illustrator II. Title.

PZ7.J38Li 2014   j823'.914   C2013-908333-2
                                       C2013-908334-0

Library of Congress
Cataloging-in-Publication Data

CIP available at Library of Congress

This story is based on the traditional fairy tale,
Little Red Riding Hood, but with a new twist.
Can you make up your own twist for the story?

Once upon a time there
was a naughty girl named
Little Bad Riding Hood.

One day, her mother said,
"Take these cakes to your granny,
dear, and try to be good.

Go straight there and don't speak to any strangers."

Little Bad Riding Hood set off,
but soon wandered off the path
and met a tall, gray stranger.
"Mmm…cakes," said the wolf.
"They look delicious."

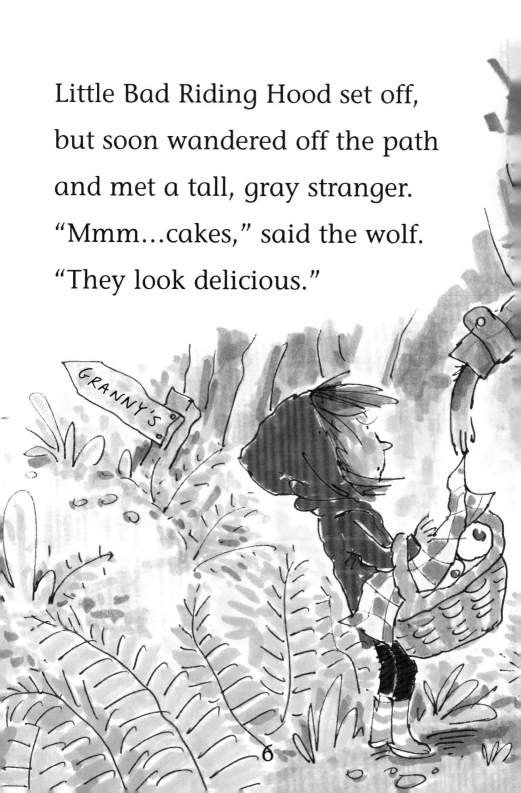

"Hands off—they're for my granny!" said Little Bad Riding Hood, trying to be good.

"But she won't miss one, will she?" said the wolf. Suddenly he heard a noise and ran off.

Little Bad Riding Hood walked on,
but thought about the wolf's words.

Mmm . . .
they   look
delicious!

GRANNY'S

She ate one
little cake...

then another...

and another!

"Oh, crumbs!" cried Little Bad
Riding Hood after she had eaten
all the cakes. "Now what can I
give Granny?"

She looked around and put
stones in her basket instead.
"Perhaps Granny won't notice,"
she thought and hurried on.

Meanwhile, at Granny's cottage, the wolf was busy. He tied Granny up and hid her.

He put on her nightcap.

He jumped into her bed.

He made up a tasty menu.

Menu
1. Cakes
2. Granny
3. Bad Riding Hood

At last there was a knock at the door. "Granny, may I come in?" called Little Bad Riding Hood.

"Yes, my dear," the wolf replied,

pretending to be Granny.

"Oh, Granny!" said Little Bad
Riding Hood. "You look very ill.
What big eyes you've got!"

"All the better to see you with,"
said the wolf. "Now give me
the cakes!"

"But Granny," said Little Bad Riding Hood, "you look terrible. What a big nose you've got!"

"All the better to smell you with," said the wolf.

Now give me the cakes.

"But Granny," said Little Bad Riding Hood, "what a big mouth you've got."
"All the better to eat you with," said the wolf.

23

"Take them," said Little
Bad Riding Hood.
"But you won't like them."
The wolf grabbed the basket
and started to eat.

25

CRACK went his teeth as they crunched on the stones!

crunch!

crack!

"OUCH!" cried the wolf
as his teeth fell out.
He ran away, toothless!

"Well done, Little Bad Riding Hood!" said Granny. "The wolf won't be eating anyone for a while. But why were you bringing me a basket of stones?"

As Granny looked around, Little Bad Riding Hood was already running out the door!

Puzzle 1

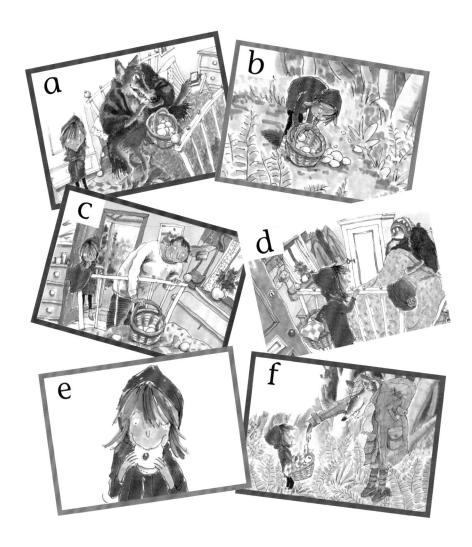

Put these pictures in the correct order. Which event is the most important? Try writing the story in your own words. Use your imagination to put your own "twist" on the story!

Puzzle 2

1. Let me out of the cupboard!

2. Your granny won't miss one cake.

3. I try to be good.

4. Who is knocking at my door?

5. Come nearer so I can see you.

6. I'm on my way to see Granny.

Match the speech bubbles to the correct character in the story. Turn the page to check your answers.

Notes for adults

TADPOLES: Fairytale Twists are engaging, imaginative stories designed for early fluent readers. The books may also be used for read-alouds or shared reading with young children.

TADPOLES: Fairytale Twists are humorous stories with a unique twist on traditional fairy tales. Each story can be compared to the original fairy tale, or appreciated on its own. Fairy tales are a key type of literary text found in the Common Core State Standards.

THE FOLLOWING PROMPTS BEFORE, DURING, AND AFTER READING SUPPORT LITERACY SKILL DEVELOPMENT AND CAN ENRICH SHARED READING EXPERIENCES:

1. **Before Reading**: Do a picture walk through the book, previewing the illustrations. Ask the reader to predict what will happen in the story. For example, ask the reader what he or she thinks the twist in the story will be.
2. **During Reading**: Encourage the reader to use context clues and illustrations to determine the meaning of unknown words or phrases.
3. **During Reading**: Have the reader stop midway through the book to revisit his or her predictions. Does the reader wish to change his or her predictions based on what they have read so far?
4. **During and After Reading**: Encourage the reader to make different connections:
   Text-to-Text: How is this story similar to/different from other stories you have read?
   Text-to-World: How are events in this story similar to/different from things that happen in the real world?
   Text-to-Self: Does a character or event in this story remind you of anything in your own life?
5. **After Reading**: Encourage the child to reread the story and to retell it using his or her own words. Invite the child to use the illustrations as a guide.

HERE ARE OTHER TITLES FROM TADPOLES: FAIRYTALE TWISTS FOR YOU TO ENJOY:

Cinderella's Big Foot	978-0-7787-0440-9 RLB	978-0-7787-0448-5 PB
Jack and the Bean Pie	978-0-7787-0441-6 RLB	978-0-7787-0449-2 PB
Princess Frog	978-0-7787-0443-0 RLB	978-0-7787-0452-2 PB
Sleeping Beauty—100 Years Later	978-0-7787-0444-7 RLB	978-0-7787-0479-9 PB
The Lovely Duckling	978-0-7787-0445-4 RLB	978-0-7787-0480-5 PB
The Princess and the Frozen Peas	978-0-7787-0446-1 RLB	978-0-7787-0481-2 PB
The Three Little Pigs and the New Neighbor	978-0-7787-0447-8 RLB	978-0-7787-0482-9 PB

VISIT WWW.CRABTREEBOOKS.COM FOR OTHER CRABTREE BOOKS.

Answers
Puzzle 1
The correct order is: 1f, 2e, 3b, 4d, 5a, 6c

Puzzle 2
Little Bad Riding Hood: 3, 6
The wolf: 2, 5
Granny: 1, 4